Praise for

When the Earth Lost its Shapes

"The vividness of imagination of author Shobha Viswanath (who could have ever thought of a sandwich that looked squished!) finds befitting support in the quirkiness of illustrator Christine Kastl's acrylic rendering of this fantastic tale (who could have thought of an Inspector Clouseau look-alike slinking away with all the shapes!)"
- Snuggle with Picture Books

"This is a delightful picture book from Chennai in India published by Karadi Tales. Children will really enjoy this heart-warming story by Shobha Viswanath enhanced by the vibrant colour illustrations in acrylic by German illustrator Christine Kastl."
- Outside In Inside Out

"I enjoyed the premise of 'even the little man can make a difference' put forth in the story as Little Dot, a tiny circle, is ultimately responsible for the shapes on Earth regaining their proper form. There was also the notion of teamwork at play, and from an educational standpoint, children deal with shapes and colors in the illustrations."
- The Turning Pages

When the Earth Lost its Shapes

Fourth Reprint September 2018

Text: Shobha Viswanath
Illustrations: Christine Kastl

Karadi Tales Company Pvt. Ltd.
3A Dev Regency, 11 First Main Road,
Gandhinagar, Adyar, Chennai 600020
Tel.: +91-44-42054243
email: contact@karaditales.com
www.karaditales.com

ISBN: 978-81-8190-192-7

Printed and bound in India by
Manipal Technologies Limited, Manipal

When the Earth Lost its Shapes

Shobha Viswanath
Christine Kastl

Once upon a time, a very long time ago, the earth lost all its shapes!

Triangles and rectangles, lines and ovals, circles and squares,
all the familiar shapes disappeared.

Some say a thief stole them. Some others say there was a fierce storm that blew all the shapes away.

But no one really knew what happened.

The earth began to look like a huge shapeless
blob filled with several shapeless things.

The egg looked scrambled.

The orange looked squeezed.

The waffle looked **bitten**

The sandwich looked squished.

The paper looked torn.

The kite looked *windswept.*

The stick looked beaten.

Everyone was worried.
It was difficult to tell things apart.

There was a lot of Confusion.

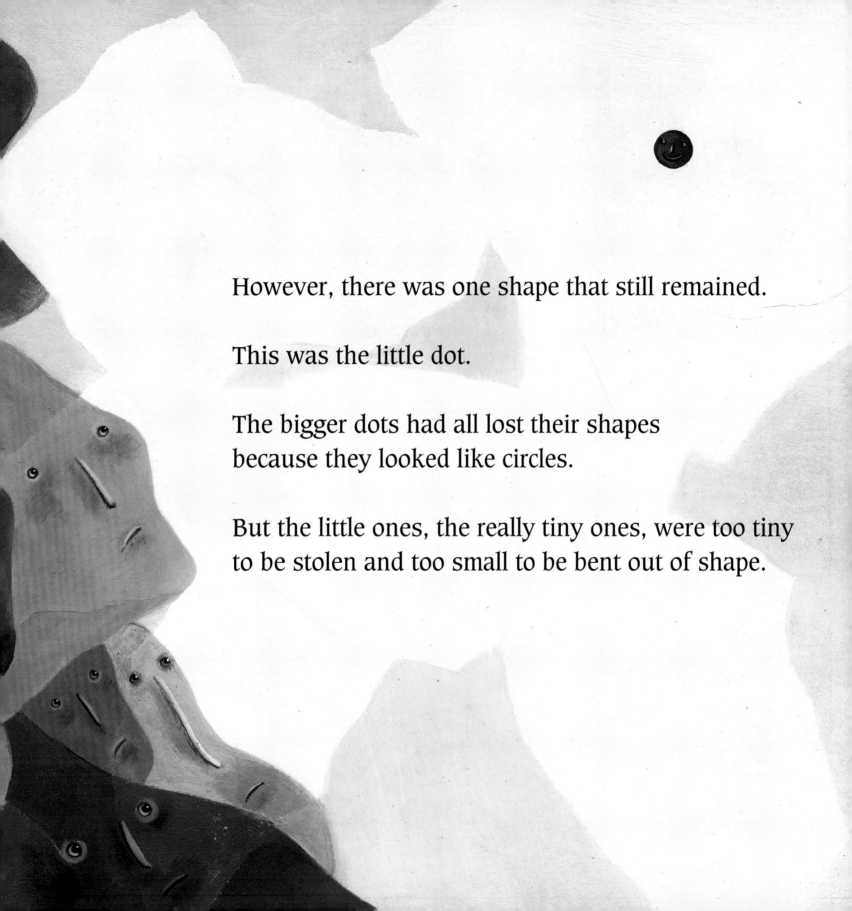

However, there was one shape that still remained.

This was the little dot.

The bigger dots had all lost their shapes
because they looked like circles.

But the little ones, the really tiny ones, were too tiny
to be stolen and too small to be bent out of shape.

'I have to do something!' thought Little Dot.

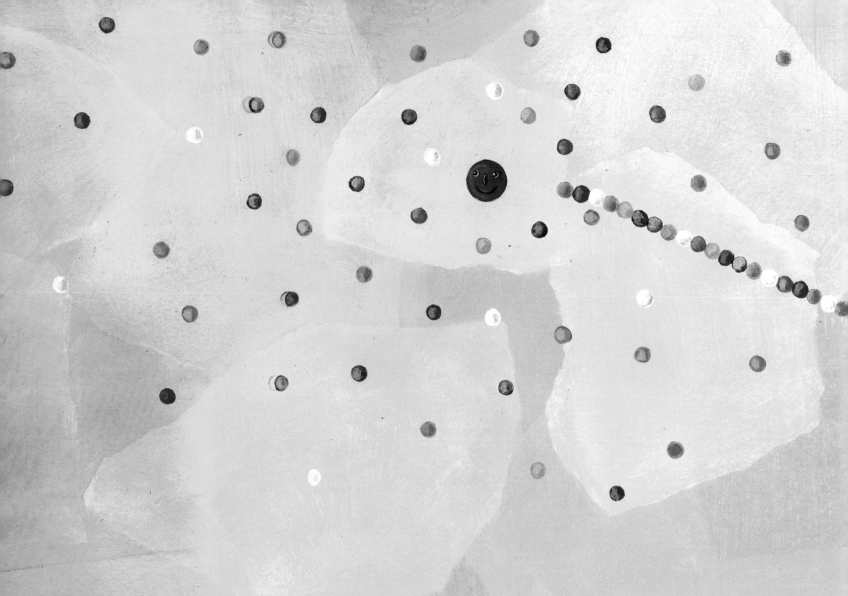

She looked for other dots like herself. There were plenty of them. Suddenly, a huge gust of wind lifted the army of dots off the ground.

"Hold on to each other," shouted Little Dot, swaying with the wind. "Hold on tight!"

The dots held on to each other.

As each dot clung to the one before it, they suddenly became a line. The wind swayed the dots this way and that, the line became wavy, and suddenly all kinds of shapes started being formed.

The wavy line twisted and turned, curved and arched, straightened and bent and soon, lo and behold! Triangles and rectangles, lines and ovals, circles and squares, all the familiar shapes reappeared.

Soon, everything was shipshape.
Everyone could tell everything apart.

The egg was oval again.

The orange was round.

The waffle was square.

The sandwich was a triangle.

The paper was a rectangle.

The kite was a diamond.

And the stick was straight as a line again.

The earth was well, happy, and in perfect shape!

Little Dot was hailed the Queen of Shapes.

And here is a secret:

If you look really closely at any shape,
you will find that it is made up of little tiny dots!

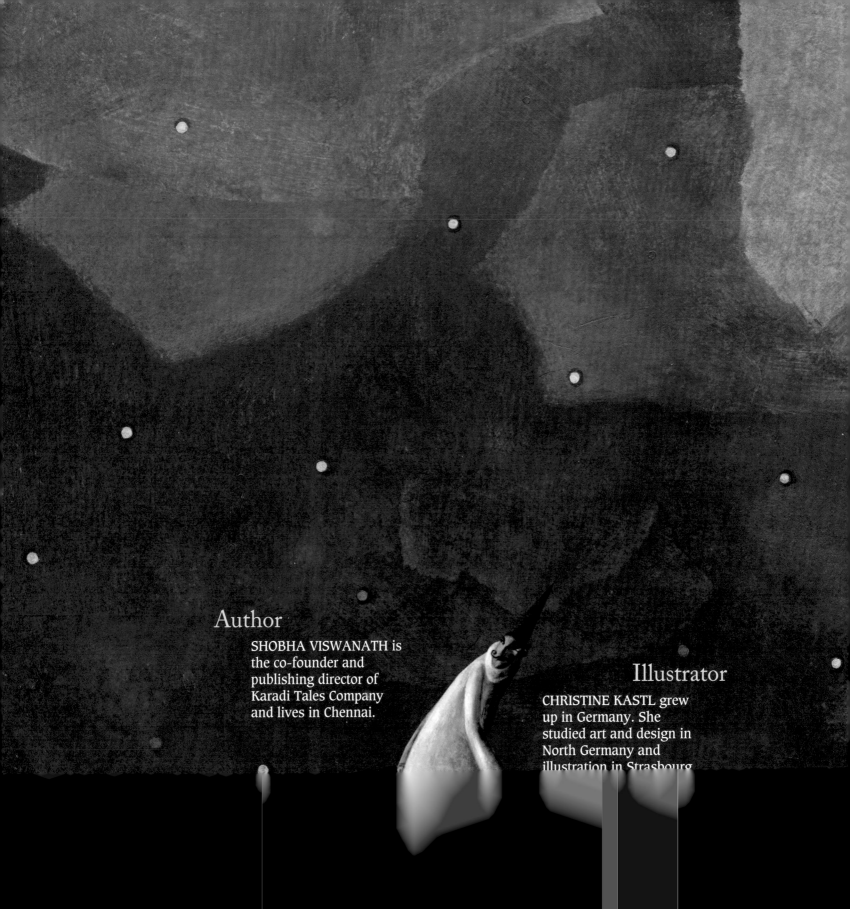

Author

SHOBHA VISWANATH is the co-founder and publishing director of Karadi Tales Company and lives in Chennai.

Illustrator

CHRISTINE KASTL grew up in Germany. She studied art and design in North Germany and illustration in Strasbourg